KV-513-467

X0000000047937

Bed time

Pippa Goodhart

Illustrated by Brita Granström

W
FRANKLIN WATTS
NEW YORK • LONDON • SYDNEY

Bed time

Bed time is full of rituals —
washing, brushing teeth and stories.
There's lots to look at and recognise here as you
follow a little girl getting ready for bed.

Jumping up the stairs
like a kangaroo.

I'm undoing three buttons.

Unbuckling two shoes.

Now I'm splashing up a storm, making lots of waves!

Weeee! Flying like a bird, flapping my wings.

Then wrapped up warm and
rub-a-dubbed dry.

I'm pulling pyjamas, POP, over my head.

I'm brushing bottom teeth,
top teeth, backs
and fronts.

Then I'm blowing hot air
to dry my hair.

And I snuggle into my dressing gown.

Cuddled up with Daddy
with his arms round about,
listening as he reads a sleepy story.

One last hug
and a kiss on the nose.

Lights out. Eyes close. Goodnight.

Sharing books with your child

Early Worms are a range of books for you to share with your child. Together you can look at the pictures and talk about the subject or story. Listening, looking and talking are the first vital stages in children's reading development, and lay the early foundation for good reading habits.

Talking about the pictures is the first step in involving children in the pages of a book, especially if the subject or story can be related to their own familiar world. When children can relate the matter in the book to their own experience, this can be used as a starting point for introducing new knowledge, whether it is counting, getting to know colours or finding out how other people live.

Gradually children will develop their listening and concentration skills as well as a sense of what a book is. Soon they will learn how a book works: that you turn the pages from right to left, and read the story from left to right on a double page. They start to realize that the black marks on the page have a meaning and that they relate to the pictures. Once children have grasped these basic essentials they will develop strategies for "decoding" the text such as matching words and pictures, and recognising the rhythm of the language in order to predict what comes next. Soon they will start to take on the role of an independent reader, handling and looking at books even if they can't yet read the words.

Most important of all, children should realize that books are a source of pleasure. This stems from your reading sessions which are times of mutual enjoyment and shared experience. It is then that children find the key to becoming real readers.

First published in 1997
This edition published 2000
by Franklin Watts
96 Leonard Street,
London EC2A 4XD

Franklin Watts Australia
14 Mars Road
Lane Cove
NSW 2066

Text copyright
© Pippa Goodhart 1997, 2000
Illustrations copyright
© Brita Granström 1997, 2000

Series editor: Paula Borton
Art director: Robert Walster

Photography Steve Shott
With thanks to Ben Ridley-Johnson

A CIP catalogue record for this
book is available from the British
Library.

ISBN 0 7496 2719 0 (hbk)
ISBN 0 7496 3486 3 (pbk)

Dewey Classification 529

Printed in Belgium

Consultant advice: Sue Robson and Alison Kelly, Senior Lecturers in Education,
Faculty of Education, Early Childhood Centre, Roehampton Institute, London.

Paperback titles in this series:

Pets	Weather	Who are you?	Time	First Experiences
Guinea Pig	Windy day	In the Sea	Morning time	New shoes
0 7496 3498 7	0 7496 3497 9	0 7496 3510 X	0 7496 3487 1	0 7496 3492 8
Kitten	Snowy day	In the Polar Lands	Play time	A party
0 7496 3499 5	0 7496 3495 2	0 7496 3511 8	0 7496 3488 X	0 7496 3491 X
Puppy	Sunny day	On the Farm	Shopping time	Staying the night
0 7496 3500 2	0 7496 3496 0	0 7496 3512 6	0 7496 3489 8	0 7496 3490 1
Rabbit	Rainy day	In the Rainforest	Bed time	Big bed
0 7496 3501 0	0 7496 3494 4	0 7496 3513 4	0 7496 3486 3	0 7496 3493 6

For Susie – PG